P9-CPZ-318

# AREN'T YOU LUCKY!

**Catherine Anholt**

JOY STREET BOOKS

Little, Brown and Company
Boston · Toronto · London

At first it was just me on my own.

Just Mommy and Daddy and me.

I didn't have a brother then.
I'd never even thought about it.

Then one day Daddy told me,
"Mommy's going to have another baby.
Aren't we lucky!"

APRIL

MAY

JUNE

JULY

AUGUST

"The baby will take a long time to
grow inside her," he said.
"We'll all have to be very patient."

SEPTEMBER

OCTOBER

NOVEMBER

DECEMBER

But I got tired of waiting.

Then at last the waiting was over.

I didn't want Mommy to leave,

but she had to go to the hospital to have the baby.

Granny stayed to look after me.

The next day we all went to visit and . . .

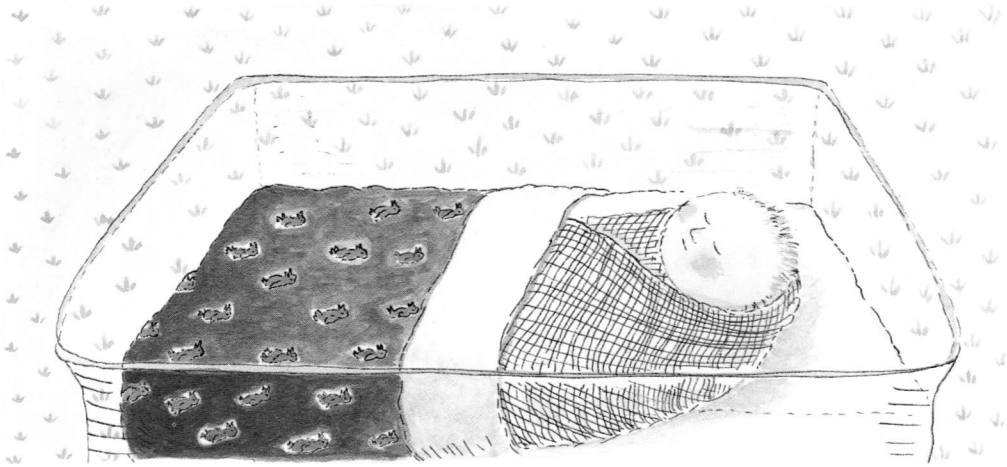

there was my little brother!

"Aren't you lucky!" said Granny.

"Do you think he looks like me or like Daddy?"
asked Mommy.
"I think he looks like a raspberry!" I said.

"Look, he's waking up now.

He can't talk yet . . .

but he can cry all right,"
Daddy said,

"especially when he's hungry."

"Can he play with me?"

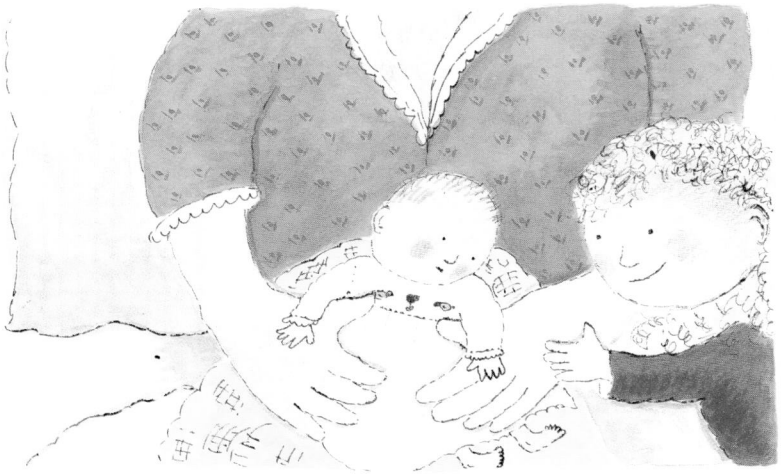

"No, he's not strong enough yet to sit up on his own."

"Hello , little baby," I said.

"I'm your sister."

Then it was me and my brother.

Mommy and Daddy, my brother and me.

Soon lots of people came to see my baby brother,

and they all said, "Aren't you lucky!"

But sometimes I didn't feel lucky at all.

It took me a long time to get used to my baby brother.

I always had to wait.

He didn't know how to play.

He cried when I made music,

but no one got upset when *he* made a noise!

Mommy asked me to try to be good but . . .

I didn't want to.

I wanted her to play with me again.

I wanted to be a baby too.

I did silly things.

One day my brother cried and cried — even during his bath.

At night Daddy said,
"Thank goodness for a little peace and quiet."

But it didn't last long!

In the end, Mommy got tired.

"I wish I had a big girl
who could help feed my baby."

"If only I had someone
who could help me," she said.

"I could do that," I said.

Then as the baby grew bigger,
we found lots of ways that I could help.

I could make him laugh.

I could brush his hair.

I could show him my books,

and do my jazzy dance for him!

There were all kinds of things that we could enjoy together.

Going for a walk.

Looking at the moon.

Having a bath,

and a bedtime hug.

Now he likes me best of all,

and whenever people see me with my little brother,
they say,

"Isn't he lucky!"